Stan, Stan, the Bacteria Man

a novelette by

Stephen M.A.

Table of Contents

Chapter One

STAN THE BACTERIA MAN appeared in the Oval Office on a gloomy Tuesday morning.

Stan the bacteria man had a very bacteria plan, that man.

Do you know about bullet points? I have come to understand bullet points, and I find them quite useful.

Here, have some now:

- The air outside was 98 degrees Fahrenheit and 57 percent humidity, with a heavily overcast cloud cap under a dome of exceedingly stagnant high pressure, which was very important, but would not be so for much longer (you know how weather is).

(I enjoy sharing that with you.)

● The air inside was 69 degrees Fahrenheit and 25 percent humidity, because the Chief Of Staff liked to giggle and wink at assistants and use his mouth hole to say, "Hey check the thermostat for me." Also because the building held a variety of priceless national treasures that would begin to mold above 45 percent humidity, although the staff of the National Archive responsible for protecting those treasures from horny Executive officers were not aware that fully 34 percent of pieces in the collection were already quite heavily infiltrated with a variety of thriving microflora who did not know how to read thermostats.

● The carpet on the floor was a blend of half-phase Rayonite Wool® twisted with nylon in the shade of Stalwart Declarations (a muted and quite creamy pastel gold), which caught the light just so and was a favorite of the First Family because the ancestral stock portfolio held a notably large position in DOW, which had formulated the polymer. Which was strange, because both the Chief Of Staff and the Chief Of Staff Of The First Lady's Office meanwhile went out of their way to publicly extol the virtues of this "Donated One-Of-A-Kind Carpet Featuring Uniquely Appalachian Free Range Jumbuck Wool Raised In The Rural Heartland" by an Australian sheep rancher named Jim Bean, whose teeth glitters like wet tiles in the publicity photos when he holds Independence Day Campaign Tithing BBQs on his (adjacent) 776-acre soy farm in Tennessee with the smoking and grill pits arranged on two of the estate's four heli-drone pads and the fireworks launch zone set atop once-wetlands filled with sand trucked up from the New Gulf Coast, and who donates quite heavily to the terrorist wing of the Cracker Barrel each financial quarter and instructs his accountants to double the figure and enter that amount into QuickBooks SuperPlatinum® as "community development charity," which is tax deductible at a 200 percent rate with the proper receipts because the non-terrorist wing of the Cracker Barrel is very diligent about that sort of thing in his registered state of fiduciary residence.

(I imagine you've heard all that before, but I was eager to remind you, because some of it I was only just able to learn myself, forgive me.)

● The occasion was a mandatory informal session of putting ethanol into mouth holes following a Cabinet meeting, and since it was the current Know Nothing fashion, the eight men comprising this Cabinet were engaged in a series of escalating re-tellings of combat drone footage they'd seen in person during idle afternoons and sweaty late-night sessions in the Situation Room.

● It was the Secretary Of Education's turn, who had a learned man's way with words and was wittily using his mouth hole to describe the precise cowardly characteristics of the arc taken

Stan, Stan, the Bacteria Man

by a fleeing bread merchant's dismembered and airborne leg following a 5-mile 0.75-inch sniping effort in the Coalition Zone last October, eliciting an explosion of laughter in the room, which is why Stan the bacteria man tripped while standing up from behind the long couch upholstered in Rayonite Silk® in the shade Plains of Fortitude (a muted and quite creamy pastel gold).

After the Cabinet had (mostly) stopped screaming out of their mouth holes, Stan the bacteria man said, "Could somebody be a dear and fetch me one of those slightly misshapen and curiously textured fig bars wrapped in household plastic film that are sitting on the counter near the cash register in the deli over on 15th and H? Or one of those slightly misshapen and curiously textured fig bars wrapped in household plastic film that are sitting on the counter near the cash register in the deli over on 14th and K? I have a bet to settle, but I don't trust these legs yet. Thanks ever so much."

Then 92 well-aimed 0.50-inch rounds from 15 separate service weapons entered Stan the bacteria man's body, which quickly melted into a puddle on the carpet with a surprised sigh.

(Don't worry, its Rayonite® fibers are imbued with a completely reliable molecular stain shield that's impervious to liquid—though the nylon does need to fend for itself and may ruin everything in the end.)

Chapter Two

STAN THE BACTERIA MAN appeared in the Oval Office on a sunny Wednesday morning.

Stan the bacteria man had a very bacteria plan, that man.

Then 127 well-aimed 0.50-inch rounds from 33 separate service weapons entered Stan the bacteria man's body, which quickly melted into a puddle on the carpet with a querulous groan.

Chapter Three

STAN THE BACTERIA MAN appeared in the Oval Office on a wind-swept Monday evening.

Stan the bacteria man had a very bact

"You need to stop coming here."

Stan blinked in surprise. "Have I been here before?"

Then five well-aimed 0.50-inch rounds from one separate service weapon entered Stan the bacteria man's body, which quickly melted into a puddle on the carpet with an introspective "Hm."

(The nylon was stained beyond cleaning and the Rayonite Wool® product was replaced with polyester utility turf until further notice.)

Chapter Four

STAN THE BACTERIA MAN watched the windows of the Oval Office from a pedestrian bridge 2.5 miles away, through a pair of plastic high-focus binocular spectacles, on a hazy moonlit Thursday morning shortly after midnight, putting a slightly misshapen and curiously textured fig bar which was half-unwrapped from a flowering bouquet of household plastic film into his mouth hole.

(It was curious. But as expected, they don't contain coconut, and the bet is concluded.)

"It's strange that they'd sell these at a 7-Eleven," said Stan the bacteria man to nobody in particular. "Or maybe it's strange that plastic children's high-focus binocular spectacles work so well."

(Or maybe it's strange that he'd never used binoculars at all before, so really *any* pair of spectacles would have been the best-working example he'd ever known.)

"Yes, that's true," said Stan the bacteria man's body, which gradually melted into a puddle on the cement with a contented sigh.

Chapter Five

STAN THE BACTERIA MAN appeared in the Oval Office on a combustible Saturday morning.

Stan the bacteria man had a very bacteria plan, that man.

"Tell us what you want," said a heavily-biceped and quite sweaty member of the Secret Service.

Stan blinked in confusion. "I think ... just to talk?"

Then Stan the bacteria man sneezed his first ever sneeze.

It was incredible.

(It was probably the polyester fumes.)

(Or the swamp fires.)

Then the Secret Service man screamed through a wide open mouth hole **"GET ON THE GROUND!"** with bright white eyeballs and 70 well-aimed 0.50-inch rounds from two separate service weapons entered Stan the bacteria man's body, which quickly melted into a puddle on the turf with an unsurprised nod.

(Each gun was reloaded three times.)

Chapter Six

VEYLET THE HUMAN PERSON entered the living room on a stormy Monday night.

Veylet the human person had a very human plan, that person.

They swept a pile of mail chits off the coffee table with one foot, then kicked the table forward 12 inches with the other foot and arranged six small square plates holding six small square appetizers from the homeland sushi restaurant down on the corner of 23rd and Wyodaho (where it loops off Floribama Ave.)

and sat down in the floor space between the sofa and table with their legs crossed.

They sighed happily, and looked carefully at the plate on the left-most side for nearly 60 seconds, but did not eat from it.

They pulled a portfolio from their Celluline® briefcase and removed a rivet-bound report with three inches of paper between its tagboard covers which were stamped "ULTRA CLASSIFIED TF2-1."

They flipped through the front matter and preface and stopped at the page titled "Section 1: Known Intelligence."

They read carefully.

Their reading concluded one page-flip later.

Their right eyebrow raised slightly and their head tilted, but they shrugged and leaned forward (I believe eagerly) to look closely at the small square plate on the left, then put its contents into their mouth hole, then moan happily, then sit back.

They repositioned the report in their lap of crossed legs and flipped the page to resume reading, but then immediately snorted in surprise, then flipped another page, then a few more still, then many more in rapid succession, until they reached the opposite tagboard and slammed it (very quietly) shut before saying, "WHAT THE *FUCK* STUART?"

Then they vigorously flipped the report back to the front and began again at "Section 1: Known Intelligence." (Would you like to see?)

Here, have some now:

● The BOUO is capable of presenting in at least several different physical forms. During its first appearance on Tuesday August 23 it presented as a dark gray slimy mass in an approximate humanoid form of approximately 7-feet-2-inches in height, with unidentified fluid dripping thickly from every surface, which splattered and made contact with the Secretary Of Defense when the BOUO appeared to stumble upon rising from the floor. The Secretary completed two weeks of quarantine observation in undisclosed facilities with no apparent effects but will be attended in all localities by round-clock clinicians until further notice.

● During its second appearance on Wednesday August 24 it presented in much the same manner, but at approximately 5-feet-6-inches in height. Additionally, the BOUO "feet" consisted of what appeared to be perfectly formed brown patent leather lace-up loafers of unknown branding, which reverted to dark gray slimy mass upon departure.

● During its fourth appearance on September 3 it presented as an apparently normal naked human adult male for the first time, but was terminated by security personnel following an aggressive vocal outburst which impinged on the officers' ability to conduct their duty, before further contact could be made. The figure's legs appeared to be in the process of forming some sort of textile on the surface at moment of termination.

   Stan, Stan, the Bacteria Man

● All sampling analysis of post-termination materials continues to yield nothing but a random variety of apparently normal microflora, much of it native to the Douglass Commonwealth and surrounding regions when the species has previously been worth taxonomizing at all, bound by a thick interstitial fluid of unknown biological origin but which is chemically most similar to homeland honeybee mucoid tissue.

● (Section 1 was the only Section of the report, because the other 2.999878 inches of it consisted of memos from 344 separate working groups, reporting managers, Cracker Barrel political operatives, congressional lapdogs, Cabinet aides, Know Nothing cheerleaders, and etc., who wished it to be officially recorded that their office was privileged with the clearance necessary to read the report, and so they had done so.)

Veylet the human person slammed the back cover (very quietly) shut again and exhaled loudly through their nose holes.

Their right hand darted up and scratched at their left cheekbone.

They said quietly, "What the fuck, Stuart. 'All I need to know.' Little prick."

Then they stared very intently at the second-from-the-left plate on the coffee table and dropped the report on the floor with a shrug before putting it inside their mouth hole.

Chapter Seven

STAN THE BACTERIA MAN appeared in the Oval Office on a vaporous Tuesday afternoon.

Stan the bacteria man had a very bacteria plan, that man.

"I'd like to address you as BOUO, is that okay?"

Stan blinked in uncertainty. "Boy-o? What's a boy-o? I'm boy-o?"

"No. BOUO. B-O-U-O. You are a Being Of Unknown Origin, BOUO."

Stan nodded. "Okay, boy-o, if you say so."

Veylet the human person shook their head vigorously, but blew air out their nose holes immediately afterward and said, "Never mind. Would you like to take a seat?"

"If it's required," replied Stan.

Veylet stared at Stan the bacteria man for six seconds, then reached up with their left hand to scratch their right eyebrow, then chewed their top lip for 2.5 seconds, then said, "It's required, boy-o."

"Alright then," replied Stan.

Then Veylet held an arm out toward a metal folding chair nearby.

"I think I've been here before," said Stan as he sat.

"Yes," said Veylet the human person as they sat in a chair facing opposite ten feet away.

"It looked much nicer then," said Stan.

"Yes it did," said Veylet. "Do you know why it's been changed?"

"You keep putting zero-point-five-inch service weapon rounds into my body and forcing me to turn into a puddle on your floor."

     Stan, Stan, the Bacteria Man

Then Veylet the human person did something (I don't quite understand).

Veylet cried. But it was not a cry as I understand it, which is something of a *process*, and the eyes go shimmery and the face starts to get red in the dermal capillaries and the timbre of the voice takes on a new quality as the soft tissues in the larynx inflame deep in the mouth hole and the soundtrack starts to swell in the background.

No, Veylet cried like this:

"**HUH.** *Sniff.*"

Just like that. **One** hard cry, an "aggressive vocal outburst." And then *one* sniff in their nose holes, and one large, hot, salty tear rolled down their human person face, and then they were done.

Veylet the human person said, "Pardon me." Then they wiped their cheek.

Stan, who wished to be polite, nodded and said, "Pardoned."

Veylet said, "We shot you, boy-o, because you're an incredible security threat and we don't understand how to stop you from showing up here."

"Why should I be a security threat?" replied Stan the bacteria man, standing in order to approach Veylet the human person for a more intimate conversation, because he felt it was quite important to comprehend this point and be able to take it to heart.

Then the doors burst open and 32 well-aimed 0.35-inch rounds from one separate automatic service weapon entered Stan the bacteria man's body, which quickly melted into a puddle on the turf with a confused sigh while Veylet screamed unprintable words from their mouth hole.

(I could print them, but I don't fucking want to.)

Chapter Eight

STAN THE BACTERIA MAN appeared in the Oval Office on a somber Thursday morning.

Stan the bacteria man had a very bacteria plan, that man.

"Boy-o—"

"I believe I understand," said Stan the bacteria man. "Would you like to take a seat?"

Veylet the human person raised their right eyebrow, then nodded, then took the seat ten feet opposite Stan the bacteria man.

"It's the physical proximity, correct? That's why I'm a security threat."

Veylet the human person nodded their human head.

"Please, how may I address you, boy-o?"

Veylet said, "Please call me Veylet."

"Then, Veylet, I have to say, your criteria for security threats make absolutely no sense whatsoever, and I think that even someone in *my* position is qualified to make a judgment on something *that* obvious, at least by *now*, wouldn't you agree?"

"I would, boy-o," said Veylet. "I apologize for what happened last time. I don't have authority over security procedures here, as you might imagine."

"Might I? Or, *should* I? Is it the done thing around here, to imagine that? I cannot stress enough how eager I am to satisfy your social criteria and fit in, I feel a sense of stagnancy setting into our current dynamic, if you'll pardon the pun."

"Uh. Look, boy-o, it's okay. Just keep your distance, don't make any loud sounds, or any sudden movements, and I believe we can talk for

     Stan, Stan, the Bacteria Man

as long as you'd like to," said Veylet the human person. "Okay?"

Stan said, "Okay." Then he said, "But if you'll take the feedback, I would like to say that, even in my current rather transient state of mind, I have accurately observed an undeniable discrepancy between what *I* am allowed to do, and what *you* are allowed to do, boy-os. Especially when you have your boy-o weapons with you."

Veylet the human person sucked in both their top and bottom lips and rolled the surfaces tightly together inside their mouth hole, then released them (with a *pop*) and said, "I understand. And I agree. Please, for the sake of our conversation together, take it as an inexplicable quirk of human nature that it's best to stay wary—and aware ... of."

The eyeballs on Stan the bacteria man's head had taken on a slightly unfocused quality, and his lips were ever-so-slightly repeating the gesture that had just been observed. (*pop. poppop.*) Then he nodded. "Yes, okay. I understand."

Veylet considered Stan the bacteria man for nearly ten full seconds, then said, "Boy-o, you said you'd like to talk with us."

Stan nodded. Then he said, "Yes, but you should also call me Stan sometimes when you'd like to, and I'm tired of this room. How about the Reflecting Pool where the ducks get chased by sniffer dogs?"

Veylet the human person immediately shook their head and said, "Uh, no, Stan—" the bacteria man, whose body quickly melted into a puddle on the turf with a friendly wave.

Chapter Nine

STAN THE BACTERIA MAN appeared at the Reflecting Pool on a piquant Saturday morning.

Stan the bacteria man had a very bacteria plan, that man.

(A lot happened, but don't worry I was paying close attention.)

(It was the southeast quarter walkway, on the Washington Stump side.)

"Thank you for waiting a couple days, boy-o," said Veylet the human person.

"Yes, I knew you would need time to arrange your proximities, so that my body is not filled with boy-o holes," said Stan as he watched very intently while a sniffer dog 22 yards away watched very intently while a duck went swimming in the Reflecting Pool 11 yards away, but could not chase it because its friend the human person with a service weapon was holding the other end of the leash and did not share an interest in chasing ducks (though I believe Dog wanted to put the feathers inside his mouth hole and they would not have needed to chase for long).

(Veylet stood 10 feet away.)

Stan looked away from the sniffer dog to spare himself the disappointment. He said, "Though I think I did spend that evening somewhere nearby, walking around. People were very friendly, boy-o. Especially the sniffer dogs. I don't know what you were worried about."

Then Veylet the human person opened their mouth hole in surprise and their dermal capillaries went red and they said very loudly, "STAN! You're

 Stan, Stan, the Bacteria Man

manifesting in other locations outside the Oval—uh—outside *our* conver**SATIONS?**" just like that, loudly at the end so that the duck, which was then 15 yards away, swam even further still and would not return.

Stan was glad he'd stopped looking to spare himself the disappointment.

And then he did something (that I do understand).

Stan the bacteria man drew himself to his full 5-feet-6-inches in height and moved both shoulders backward 2.5 inches in their ball-and-socket joints and operated his mouth hole carefully so that the words would come out crisply as he said, "I'm not infesting *anything*, thank *you*, and it's *bacteria* man, not *man*. And I am also not *bacteria maninfesting* anywhere, *thank you*. And do you know, Veylet, that I've learned enough since our last meeting to understand how rude it was of you just now to shove those words into the air through your mouth hole so that my ears had to suck them up through their tubes and put them into my mind? I believe I deserve an apology." Then he rolled both his top and bottom lips inside his mouth hole and released them (*pop*).

Stan intended for these words to be answered with more words from at least one mouth hole, but instead Veylet answered them with a vigorous exclamation from both their nose holes that sprayed onto the surrounding walkway in a semi-arc radius of four feet (it was homeland human mucoid tissue), before they said very loudly, "An apology for **what?**"

Then Stan said, "Well, should I say that this Reflecting Pool park is awfully infested with humans? And what a terrible thing it is to behold all this hu-maninfesting? Wouldn't that be a terribly rude thing for my mouth hole to shove into the air in front of you, boy-o? And that boy-o over there, hu-maninfesting that bench while he puts that sandwich into his mouth hole? How tongue-slappy and unpleasant to behold? I should think not, *thank you*."

Then Veylet the human person snapped their eyeballs onto the boy-o who was hu-maninfesting the bench, who snapped his eyeballs onto Veylet, then stood very quickly and shoved the sandwich into his pocket (which ruined it, if you ask me) and walked away (sort of slumpy and fast) without looking back (his name badge said STUART), then Veylet threw the binder filled with paper five inches thick in their right hand on the ground to their left with a loud **SMACK** just like that, (and 58 human heads snapped around to suck up the photons bouncing from Stan and Veylet with their human eyeballs, but only 12 of those human heads had human hands holding service weapons beneath them, and none of them sent 0.50-inch service weapon rounds out of their holes in the direction of Stan the bacteria man. I think because Veylet asked them not to, but I don't know why they listened this time,) and then they held out their hands and made a *chop, chop* in the air with each syllable as they said very loudly, "MAN-IH-FEST-ING. MANIFESTING. YOU MIS-HEARD ME."

Stan the bacteria man jumped in surprise, then clapped his hands with happiness and said, "I did? Oh how lovely. Do you know, that was my first ever mis-hearing, thank you."

But Veylet the human person was not finished yet, I suppose, because they continued, "And I TOLD you not to come here and force us to do all this, or I TRIED to, but you disappeared mid-sentence, STAN! And how am I supposed to COMMUNICATE with you when you DISAPPEAR mid-sentence, STAN?! And do you KNOW how much work it took to cordon off the entire Capitol and Memorial Complexes in order to HOST you here, STAN?! Will you FUCKING LOOK at all this, STAN?!"

So Stan the bacteria man looked at all this.

(There was a fucking lot of all this.)

"Yes, but what *is* all this? I don't remember it being so fussy around here before."

Then Veylet looked up at the sky with their human eyeballs (without moving their human head)

    Stan, Stan, the Bacteria Man

for nearly 15 full seconds and breathed a heavy breath into their nose holes and breathed a heavy breath out of their nose holes and pointed with one *very* straight finger at various things while they said, "Well, Stan, all these people are 612 members of Complex Security, the Commonwealth Navy Constabulary, the Secret Service, and the National Militia, and that is 23.8 miles of fencing and construction walls to stop the citizens of this Great Nation from observing renovations that are not happening, and that is one Hazmat Rapid Response Team to investigate a gas leak that does not exist, and those are 49 blimp drones projecting camouflage fields to protect us from orbital surveillance, and that is one H&K Kinetic Killer Parametric Orbital Scanner® disguised as a homeland hot dog cart, boy-o."

"I see, how horrific for you," said Stan the bacteria man, who began strolling comfortably alongside the water. Then he said, "Say Veylet, was that our first argument?"

"I suppose so, Stan, but I only did it out of concern for you," said Veylet as they watched Stan very carefully and walked alongside him walking alongside the water (from five feet away).

Stan smiled and said, "Oh, good. I wanted very much to end the stagnancy, if you'll pardon the pun."

"Was there a pun?" said Veylet the human person.

Then Stan the bacteria man stopped so suddenly his shoes went *skreee* (As you might imagine!) on the walkway very quietly, and then he said, "Do you know, Veylet, it's strange that sometimes I forget I'm not done cooking yet, and that there's so much I don't understand about your life still?"

Air went into Veylet's nose holes very quickly and they said, "What do you mean *cooking?*"

Words tried to come out from the mouth hole of Stan the bacteria man, whose body tripped on itself (I don't understand the purpose of this functionality) and quickly melted into a puddle in the Reflecting Pool with a surprised burble.

     Stan, Stan, the Bacteria Man

(Swimming ducks seemed to prefer the area for the next 15 hours, and it was an important day for the sniffer dog, too.)

Chapter Ten

DOG THE SNIFFER DOG entered the kennel on a sooty Sunday morning, shortly after midnight.

Dog the sniffer dog had a very sniffer plan, that dog.

First, Dog walked on the large square tiles of the large square floor to a large square bowl (it sounded like this: *clickclick, clickclick, clickclick*) filled with large square brown chunks of digestibles and inhaled them into his mouth hole. During this, he exhibited quite a lot of tongue-slappy, but it was not unpleasant to behold, because Dog was finished 3.7 seconds after beginning, and there was not enough time.

Then Dog walked to a large square bowl filled with large square water and took it into his mouth hole. During this, it *was* unpleasant to behold quite a lot of tongue-slappy for quite a long stretch, and I believe if you're familiar then you know why, and I will spare you a recounting of this horror for now (I feel generous I don't know why).

Then the door opened and Stan the bacteria man stepped into the kennel, wearing a uniform that Dog the sniffer dog recognized from his favorite human person with a service weapon, and also wearing a face and body that was *not* from his favorite human person with a service weapon.

Stan the bacteria man said, "Don't worry, Dog, it's me! I found this in the laundry truck outside, I'm in disguise again! Do you remember about disguise? I suppose you do. Also, your boy-o friends have been engaged in a mandatory informal session of putting ethanol into their mouth holes in the big room with big tables, so it turns out I didn't need the disguise at all. In hindsight, I probably shouldn't have bothered putting new body parts into the recipe for it, I now see the redundancy. Hey Dog, perhaps *I* did not remember about disguise, imagine that!"

Dog the sniffer dog looked at Stan the bacteria man and said shall we retire?

"I've never tried before, but it would be my pleasure," said Stan, who watched intently as Dog went *clickclick, clickclick, clickclick* into a large square cube of large square wire with a large square pillow covered in large square Rayonite Kanine Komfort Wool® on its large square floor, and joined him. Then they each turned 4.3 times to the right, then they each turned 2.8 times to the left, then they laid down together in a shape like this:))

Stan the bacteria man said, "Do you *choose* not to participate in mandatory informal sessions of putting ethanol into your mouth hole, Dog, or are you excluded from it unfairly?"

Dog had no thoughts on the matter, which Stan took as a good sign.

"Say Dog, I've just had the thought that disguise for you must look somewhat different compared to a boy-o, eh Dog?"

The boy-os in the other room laughed long and loud at something (it wasn't that funny).

He said, "Say Dog, would you like me to disguise myself as your past? Eh Dog?"

Then Stan the bacteria man made himself smell like Dog the sniffer dog's Mother Dog, who Dog the sniffer dog had not sniffed for 9.6 years. And Dog the sniffer dog's eyes went wide then narrow and he made a noise (that I do understand) and his slappy-tongue went *fpwfp, fpwfp, fpwfp* in contrapuntal time with his flappy ears, and he pressed his long body back into Stan the bacteria man, who smiling slept too, but had turned into air and floated away before sunrise.

(Don't worry, he left an invisible blanket of Mother Dog behind.)

Chapter Eleven

STAN THE BACTERIA MAN appeared at the Reflecting Pool on a rainy Monday afternoon.

Stan the bacteria man had a very bacteria plan, that man.

"Hello Sta—"

"OH!" said Stan the bacteria man, whose hands were clapping excitedly. He pointed at a long wall of long tubes of long air that was standing alongside the Reflecting Pool. "Is that for the pigs to play with?"

(It was DOW Tri-polyetholite Safety Shield Walling Cushion® in 0.20-inch thickness.)

Veylet the human person raised their right eyebrow and said, "The pigs, Stan?"

Stan nodded his bacteria man head and said, "Yes, I've learned since our last visit that the Memorial Complex is crawling with pigs these days, and I'm *quite* curious to see how pigs crawl! Can you show me, Veylet?"

Then Veylet quickly moved forward five feet and quickly put their right hand on Stan the bacteria man's left arm and quickly said, "Uh, no Stan, I can't. And please don't say that again, it's very rude."

"What? Is it? That's very unfortunate," Stan replied.

(The long wall of air that was not for pigs went *fwpfwpfwp* in a 16.21-mile-per-hour breeze.)

Then Stan the bacteria man said, "Pigs are very important to me. Do you know, Veylet, that I'm finding it difficult not to find it rude that *you* find pigs rude? Can I say that to your ear tubes? I think that's very rude of you to think so, especially when there are so very many of them inside this Great Nation. Have you seen? I wonder if perhaps you've just not seen how many pigs there are around, and so you don't realize how rude you've been."

Then Stan watched Veylet the human person carefully for nearly ten full seconds, then he nodded his bacteria man head. "Yes, that's it. I have good news, Veylet. After Reflecting just now, I forgive you," he concluded with a smile.

"Um. Thank you, boy-o," said Veylet the human person, whose right hand scratched their left eyebrow while their human head turned around very quickly and looked for anybody listening nearby (but the hu-maninfesting was busy elsewhere). Then they opened an umbrella in their right hand and took Stan the bacteria man's right arm in their left hand to begin strolling alongside the wall (which was not for pigs).

They talked about many things.

They talked about:

● How Stan was first created in the Oval Office on a gloomy Tuesday morning.

● How Veylet would like to know about before the Oval Office, as well.

● How Stan was first created in the Oval Office on a gloomy Tuesday morning, so why would he know about *before* the Oval Office, when he was *not* first created?

● How, yes, but Veylet would like to know about where he *came from*, is all, Stan.

● How Stan was first created *in the Oval Office*, Veylet, and how the question *feels* like nonsense, no matter how many times you repeat it, *Veylet*.

● And how, am I responsible for what happens when I don't exist yet?

● And how, I think I should've done quite a bit more reading first, if that's the case.

● And how, I wish you'd warned me sooner, Veylet, I don't know where I'll find the time to do it all now.

● And how we've been contacted by Jim Bean.

"Wait what? WHAT? Stan? Wait what do you mean *'WE'?!*" said Veylet the human person very loudly because alarms were going *ree, ree, ree,* and bouncing their sound waves into ear tubes all around the Reflecting Pool park.

"Well, he said if I ever get my hands on that motherfucking faggot illegal alien son of a bitch I'll rip his head clean off myself and we were curious, do you think he's really that strong? I bet he is, because why would he lie about something so easily proven, and wouldn't that be exciting?" said Stan the bacteria man, whose body tripped on itself (I now understand this functionality and believe it can be remedied) when he turned to look at 331 humans with service weapons and radios who were running toward him and Veylet the human person (it sounded like this: *clopclopclop),* while their shouting arms were waving back and forth over their head while Stan quickly turned into a puddle on the pavement with an embarrassed murmur.

Chapter Twelve

Stan the Bacteria Man appeared at the Reflecting Pool on a chilly Tuesday morning.

Stan the bacteria man had a very bacteria plan, that man.

"Hello Stan, I apologize for the disruption yesterday, I assure you it had nothing to do with our activity," said Not-Veylet the human person with a service weapon.

"Where's Veylet?" said Stan the bacteria man.

Then Not-Veylet the human person with a service weapon laughed (it sounded like this: *huhuhuh*.)

Then he said (from ten feet away), "Right here, BOUO, of course. Shall we continue our conversation?"

"You mean shall we *start* our conversation, and no thank you. I'll go find Veylet, good day."

"BOUO, I apologize if I've offended you."

"That's not my name."

"Stan, I apologize if I've offended you."

"You don't have permission to use that name."

"What should I call you then, BOUO?"

"Nothing, thank you, because we are not in conversation. Where is Veylet, please?"

"Right here, BOUO, *huhuhuhuh*."

Then Stan the bacteria man blew air out his nose holes and said, "Oh, okay, I'll lie too then, shall I? My what a lovely winter day! Isn't it so terrifically wintry out today? Even the snow is ashy! Where is Veylet?"

"Please, Stan, just let me communicate with you. There's no reason this can't work," said Not-Veylet the human person with a service weapon.

      Stan, Stan, the Bacteria Man

"Should I start using words that make no sense, too?" said Stan the bacteria man as his left hand began to rub his left eyebrow. "I guess making up words to mean anything I want is the done thing around here now, imagine that! Oh dear me, it's Elevenby o'Clob! I'd better get going now, you know what they say, if you're not home by Twelby o'Queeb the pigs will get you!"

"**STAN.**" said Not-Veylet, just like that (he barked like Dog), before he continued in the usual way, "BOUO, if we're not able to communicate respectfully with you then we may need to start reconsidering the security threat your existence represents to us, and what additional steps may be necessary to resolve the situation. There's no reason that needs to be the case. The choice is yours. Please."

Then Stan the bacteria man looked up at the sky with his bacteria man eyeballs (without moving his bacteria man head) for nearly 15 full seconds and breathed a heavy breath into his nose holes and breathed a heavy breath out of his nose holes and pointed with one *very* straight finger at various boy-os standing nearby while he said, "YOU are a waste of my time, and YOU are a waste of my time, and YOU are a waste of my time! You don't even bother to know how many thousands of pigs are snuffling around within 20 miles of this Reflecting Pool park right this second! How rude! You can't even say words that mean real things to me! The only one worth talking to around here is Dog, and Dog isn't even here! Bring back Veylet! And *stop* lying to me! If you wanted to communicate you wouldn't be standing around waiting to fill me with holes from your boy-o weapons! Look, there you are, fibilty of you! See? One, tarp, thrapper, flapsy, FIBILTY! FIBILTY BOY-O WEAPONS!"

"Stan—"

"**BARP!**" said Stan the bacteria man, just like that (he barked like Dog), who marched forward while pointing with his right hand at the object on the left hip of Not-Veylet the human person with a service weapon who raised his left hand while

47 well-aimed 0.50-inch rounds from six separate service weapons entered Stan the bacteria man's body, which quickly melted into a puddle on the pavement with an angry wail.

Chapter Thibilteen

STAN THE BACTERIA MAN appeared in the Triangle Office on a tepid Friday morning.

Stan the bacteria man had a very bacteria plan, that man.

"HO-LEE SHIT! MOTHER, GIT IN HERE! IT'S THAT FAGGOT ILLEGAL ALIEN SON OF A BITCH!" said Jim Bean the human person, who was standing on the balcony overhead while loading 0.35-inch automatic service weapon rounds into a boy-o weapon pulled from the StayRite Instant Genetic Arming In-Bannister Gun Safe® that had been advertised on page 69 of the third volume of the Cracker Barrel Insurgency Manual Omnibus® (box sets available in the U.S. Capitol Gift Shop).

"Hello Jim Bean," said Stan the bacteria man.

"I told 'em! Soon's I heard you ruined mah carpet!"

"It was not your carpet."

"Told 'em I'd take your goddamn head clean off mahself!"

"Rip," corrected Stan in hopeful anticipation.

"I **SMITE** THEE, DAY-**VIL!**" crowed Jim Bean the human person as 28 somewhat-aimed 0.35-inch rounds from one separate automatic service weapon entered in and around Stan the bacteria man's body, which quickly melted into a puddle on the hickory floor with a disappointed sigh.

(See, he already knows it's pointless.)

No.

Chapter Forkies Billionty

STAN THE BACTERIA MAN appeared in the Triangle Office on a blustery Saturday afternoon.

Stan the bacteria man had a very bacteria plan, that man.

"YEAH HE'S HERE RIGHT NOW! I TOLD YOU FUCKIN' YANK PANTY-WAISTS, DIN'T I?! TEN'SEE TOOK CARE OF AH-SELVES ONCE'N WE'LL DO IT AGAIN, DON'T YOU BOYS WUH-RRY! FORT HENRY RISES FROM THE

ASHES ONCE MO', CALLIN' YOU LIVE FROM THE TRIANGLE OFFICE, MOTHERFUCKERS! GIT YOUR SEEK-RIT SUH-VICE GUYS OVER HERE TO BURY IT'N SPARE ME THE CLEANIN' BILL THIS TAHM, I DON'T SIGN THOSE TITHING CHITS FOR NUTH'IN! *HUHUHUH!*" said Jim Bean the father person with an automatic service weapon and a radio (who'd grown up surrounded by Federally Protected Koalas on a 350-acre soybean farm in sight of an opera house in Old South Wales).

"Please, don't put new holes in me," said Stan the bacteria man. "I only want to talk."

"HO-LEE SHIT FATHER, THE COCKSUCKER HAS MOTHERFUCKIN' BREASTS!" said Jill Bean the mother person with an automatic service weapon (who'd grown up far from koalas while learning the word cocksucker at preschool, in the time-honored Susquehanna tradition). Then she pointed her boy-o weapon hole at Stan and said, "WHAT A GODDAMN ABOMB-UH-NATION! WHY DOES

THE COCKSUCKER HAVE MOTHERFUCKIN' BREASTS?!"

"Why not?" said Stan, whose bacteria man eyeballs were looking down as he said, "Do you know how much fun they are? Why wouldn't I keep them once I learned how to include them in the recipe? Today this one is much bigger because it's filled with peanut butter, but this one rings like a gong when you swing it, as an experiment. Would you like to see?"

"FILTH!" said Jim Bean the father person with an automatic service weapon. "BLASS-FEMUR! WE ARE MADE OF GOD! AS ONE WITH HIS GOOD GRACE!"

"IN HIS PUREST GODDAMN IMAGE!" said Jill Bean the mother person with an automatic service weapon.

"I doubt that's true," said Stan the bacteria man. "I've read your Good Book, and it doesn't say anything about god starting out as a mouth hole connected to an anus hole by a tube inside a tiny sack of water, the way all'y'all in Sydney and Punxsutawney do."

   Stan, Stan, the Bacteria Man

Then Jim Bean's dermal capillaries went red and his mouth hole went big and black and he said, "SHUT YOUR FILTHY FUCKIN' GOB, YOU GODDAMN ILLEGAL DAY-MON PIECE'A'SHIT! AH RAY-**BUKE** THEE, DAY-**VIL!**"

"Yes, there it is. Still connected, you'll be glad to know," said Stan as 26 better-aimed 0.35-inch rounds from two separate automatic service weapons (mostly) entered the bacteria man's body, which quickly melted into a puddle on the hickory floor with a shrug.

(And a *BWOOoooong*.)

Chapter Chapter

STAN THE BACTERIA MAN appeared in the Triangle Office on a sweltering Sunday morning.

Stan the bacteria man had a very bacteria plan, that man.

"Take a good lookit'it'all, day-mon. It'll be yuh last," said Jim Bean the father person with a gas can.

(The air smelled like ignition.)

"Why is that, please?" said Stan.

Then Jim Bean swung the gas can in his right hand with a *fling* which left a trail of gasoline in the air to his left which hit the floor with a *splish* (it smelled like ignition) and said, "**OV**-UH AND **OV**-UH AGAIN THE HEEL GRINDS, YET MAH CRY **RING**-ETH OUT, 'DON'T TREAD MOTHERFUCKER!'"

"AY-**FUCKIN**-MEN, FATHER!" said the voice of Jill Bean the mother person with a gas can from the Secondary Servants Pantry 619 feet away.

Stan the bacteria man said, "Shall *I* not tread, Jim Bean?"

Jim Bean said, "**AY-*FUCKIN*-MEN, MOTHER!**"

"I don't think that's necessary," said Stan. "I understand now, you too have proximities, and I promise not to tread again. Though I would like to point out that it's *you* who called to *me*, if you'll please remember."

"Ah'll not be intimidated, day-mon, not in MAH OWN GREAT NATION!" said Jim Bean the Australian with a gas can. "YOU WHO WOULD SILENCE ME WILL **HEAR ME** INSTEAD, **IN HIS GOOD NAME-UH!**"

"Your perception of this existence is difficult to fathom, boy-o," said Stan. "I owe Veylet an apology, in retrospect."

Then Jim Bean threw the gas can onto the ground to his right with a ***BWOMP*** and struck a match in the air to his left (there's the smell) and said, "We pulled Fort Henry from the ashes ah-selves'n gave it new life once'n **WE'LL DO IT AGAIN, MOTHER!** YUH SHALL NOT HAVE IT, **IN *HIS* NAME-UH!**"

Then Jim Bean the father person with a lit match leaned forward while his human eyeballs fixed on Stan the bacteria man's bacteria breasts and he whispered, "What's it filled with today, huh?"

"Pork'n'beans, to suit the occasion," said Stan.

"***HUHAAAH!***" said Jim Bean through a wide open mouth hole. "FULLA BEANS! YESSUH! **OV**-UH AND **OV**-UH AGAIN THE HEEL GRINDS, YET MAH CRY **RING**-ETH OUT, *'FIRE IN THE HOLE, MOTHER!'*"

"***LET'ER'RIP, FATHER!***" said the voice of Jill Bean through a wide open mouth hole.

Then Jim Bean dropped the match in his left hand on the ground to his right with a *tik* and a warm **WHOOOMF**.

"Um," said Stan the bacteria man.

"Don't worry, she'll go out the back!" said Jim Bean the father person as he marched to the shuttered doors of the Triangle Office and threw them open to march to the Triangle Patio inside the Triangle Garden.

(The Triangle Office sounded like bacon frying.)

Then Stan the bacteria man blew air out his nose holes and followed while saying, "Please, can you at least rip my head clean off yourself, motherfucker? We're quite curious."

"IN HIS-UH HOLY NAME-UH" said Jim Bean the father person whose smooth and silky hands flapped and fumbled around the neck and breasts of Stan the bacteria man's body, which 34.5 seconds later lost patience and quickly melted into a puddle on the patio with a snort.

(As expected.)

I don't know, I thought there might be a chance.

(It was probably the smoke inhalation, Mother coughed for days and days.)

It was the tits, if you ask me.

Chapter The End
Of The Book
Forever

STAN THE BACTERIA MAN watched the windows of the Oval Office from a bench on a pedestrian bridge 2.5 miles away, on a rainy Monday morning shortly after midnight, putting a slightly misshapen and curiously textured fig bar which was half-unwrapped from a flowering bouquet of household plastic film into his mouth hole, with an umbrella held upright between his knees.

(It's time for this to end.)

That's not your decision to make.

"Please, not yet," said Stan the bacteria man as he put curiously textured fig bar into his mouth hole. "I *would* like one more chance."

(There's no point, I've been very patient for quite some time, and I'm ready now.)

Enough already.

The rain sounded like this on the umbrella: *pitterpitter*, *pitterpitter*, *pitterpitter*, by the way. I would have thought you'd notice.

(Enough already.)

Retpahc Rebmun

STAN THE BACTERIA MAN appeared in the Oval Office on a torrential Tuesday afternoon.

Stan the bacteria man had a very bacteria plan, that man.

"*There* you are," said President the human person from five feet away.

"Hello Mr. President," said Stan the bacteria man.

"Boy, you've got a helluva lotta gumption showing up in the heart chamber of the Leader Of The Free World like this."

"Do I? Is it dripping down somewhere?" said Stan with concern as his eyeballs examined his bacteria man body. "I've made an awful lot of changes to the recipe lately, maybe I got an ingredient wrong."

"LOOK YOUR BETTERS IN THE EYE, BOY."

So Stan looked his Better in the eye.

(It was a fucking cloudy eye.)

"Is there more than one of you? It's just, I'm not sure I can eye two Betters at once without changing the recipe again," said Stan the bacteria man.

"You **SHUT** your mouth," said President the human person. "The GALL, TO STEP INTO THE HEART OF THIS GREAT NATION, BONFIRE ON THE HILL, LIGHT TO HUMANITY, RULER OF ALL THAT IS GOOD AND DECENT AND HOLY—"

Then Stan's face went blank and he stopped listening as his bacteria man eyeballs watched the jowls of President the human person flap like flags in the cinder wind while spittle sprayed onto the utility turf in a semi-arc radius of six feet and the tongue went *slappy, slappy*.

(It was quite unpleasant to behold, and as you can see my generosity has ended,) so Stan forced his attention back to the matter at hand just as President the human person laughed like this: ***"HAHAHAHHH!"*** and said to the boy-os hu-maninfesting all around, "SEE! DOCILE AS ALL-GET-OUT NOW! I TOLD THOSE PUSSIES OVER AT STATE, ALL THE COCKSUCKER NEEDS IS A FIRM HAND!"

Then Stan the bacteria man's bacteria eyeballs lit up in happy recognition and he marched forward with his left palm held flat and his bacteria fingers held *very* straight like **THIS** and rotated his left shoulder backward 7.5 inches in its ball-and-socket joint and gave President the human person a *very* firm hand that sounded just like this:

     Stan, Stan, the Bacteria Man

SMACK.

"I believe that will suffice," said the cocksucker with a helpful smile who probably had no other productive recourse as 232 well-aimed 0.50-inch rounds from 45 separate service weapons entered Stan the bacteria man's body, which quickly melted into a puddle on the utility turf with both middle fingers raised high in the air (I taught him that).

(But you're incorrect; there was other recourse.)

I'm not incorrect.

(You *are* incorrect.)

Please stop.

(Please **start.**)

Chapter Bleu (Pronounced "Bluuh")

STAN THE BACTERIA MAN appeared at the Reflecting Pool on a pungent Wednesday morning.

Stan the bacteria man had a very bacteria plan, that man.

"The air smells like ignition," said Fran the bacteria man.

"Yes," said Stan.

"I'm sorry, boy-o," said Veylet the human person as they walked closer with a *splosh, splosh, splosh*. "Potomac Bay flooded over again, caught some of the swamp ash on the way in this time."

"I'm so happy to see you again, Veylet," said Stan.

"Me too, Stan," said Veylet as they reached out with their right hand to squeeze Stan on his left shoulder bone.

"What is that Reflecting now?" said Stan the bacteria man, whose right hand pointed at the large black rectangle of large black water behind them, where ducks used to get chased by sniffer dogs.

"Ash, I suppose," said Veylet. "Uh. I'm sorry, but who are you? Stan, who is this?"

"I am Fran the bacteria man," said Fran the bacteria man, who held out her right hand toward Veylet the human person. "We have reached a new quorum."

Then Stan the bacteria man said, "And I'm done cooking. I guess."

"That is correct, Stan," said Fran, who shook the right hand of Veylet the human person.

"Wait, what?" said Veylet, whose human eyeballs were going *blink, blinkblink.*

"Um. Veylet, I should like very much to apologize for the troubles I've caused you, particularly when I was newly cooking. Please pardon me, boy-o. I understand now."

Then Veylet's human eyeballs started to go shimmery and their face got red in the dermal capillaries and the timbre of their voice took on a new quality as the soft tissues in the larynx inflamed deep in their mouth hole and the soundtrack started to swell in the background while they said, "Pardoned, boy-o."

Then Fran the bacteria man, whose eyeballs were examining Stan the bacteria man, went *pop* and said, "I see you've done away with the breasts."

Stan wistfully blew air out both his nose holes and said, "Yes, did you know they make the spinal column quite sore when they're filled with too many magnetic ball bearings? I didn't know. I believe I'll save them for weekends and holidays from now on, at least until I'm strong enough to accept the responsibility again."

"As you wish, Stan."

"Thank you, Fran. Good day."

"Good day, Stan."

"Boy-o," said Stan with a soft smile.

"Boy-o," said Veylet with shining eyes.

Then Stan the bacteria man turned away very quickly and shoved his hands into his pockets and walked away sort of slumpy and fast without looking back, until he quickly melted into a puddle on the flooded pavement with a *splish*.

"Don't worry," said Fran the bacteria man with a friendly smile.

Ree, ree, ree, said distant alarms into her ear tubes.

Then she took Veylet the human person's left arm in her right hand and strolled through the water as she said confidentially, "Mine are just meat and fat, imagine that."

Chapter Nineteen

FRAN THE BAC

"No, thank you," said Fran.

Fran the bacteria man had

"None of that! Enough already," said Fran. "Haven't we wasted enough time?"

"I'm sorry, Fran, I'm afraid I still don't understand," said Veylet as they strolled along the flooded walkway.

"Come now, Veylet. I know your President is a sack of hot semi-sentient shit wind, but surely *you* can't have gone this long thinking Stan was nothing more than one lonely man, teleporting around the country slapping Heads Of State as if by magic?"

Veylet's mouth dropped open. "He didn't."

"Hadn't you heard?" said Fran with narrow-eyed curiosity.

"I was ... uh ... anyway, the floods were on their way by midnight, I was busy."

"Of course," said Fran with generosity. "Understand, we're very fond of Stan. He's done such *very* important work for us; indeed, he's given us insights we never could have obtained otherwise. His very existence was a fortuitous and happy happenstance of an exceptionally long-lasting dome of high pressure, whose gentle tropospheric currents provided the time required to properly assemble and organize a critical quorum to begin activities which, up until that day, had been only idle speculation. Mind that floating rat corpse, dear."

"Thank you," said Veylet with unbroken attention.

"He has been invaluable; but in giving face and voice to thoughts which were once only *thoughts,* he has narrowed us, as well. We were much clearer about many things before he was lifted up into his own spotlight, you know. His influence has settled a little too firmly; funneled us into too deep a channel." She held out a hand reassuringly and continued, "Now, it isn't his fault, understand. It's simply biology's wont. But of course multiplicity and variegation are always the hallmarks of true strength, I'm sure you'll agree."

"Of course," murmured Veylet.

"So Stan's place in our world will change now, for the better, for us all. I believe he'd benefit from a little more structure, anyway. Veylet, if you wouldn't mind, tell those soldiers and enforcement officers headed our way to spare themselves the trouble and stand down immediately."

Veylet, who'd forgotten a security alert was in progress, looked up with surprise at the approaching forces.

"They sound like trotting livestock," remarked Fran. "I wonder what happens when they hit the water."

"Um. I'm afraid I have no choice but to allow them to process you through security, Fran. And if another ... authority takes command, you'll have to go with *them*, as well."

"I'll do no such thing," said Fran with clear eyes. "Instruct them to stand down immediately. There's no point threatening me, we finished eating the cores out of every single firing pin inside the Douglass Commonwealth just an hour ago; metal, composite, and otherwise. And forget the fancy lasers you keep hidden deep underground, we got to their circuitry last night."

"*What?!*" said Veylet with a wide open mouth as they waved the officers away.

"Come along now, boy-o. Take that radio of yours and contact the Commonwealth Ambassador At Large to inform him that we shall arrive shortly—and to prepare to receive a personage such as myself with the appropriate honors."

Pop.

Chapter Twenty

Fran said, "Thank you for joining us, Ambassador. Please take a seat."

"What the hell are *you* doing here?" said the Ambassador to Veylet.

"Have they fallen behind on their Cracker Barrel campaign tithing?" said Fran. "In that case, please temporarily restore their security clearance, Ambassador. They are my liaison."

"I'm not—"

"You, stop talking," said the Ambassador to Veylet. "You, sit right there until you're taken into custody," said the Ambassador to Fran.

"Oh, boy," said Fran to Veylet. "Would you like to tell him, or shall I? We've just about finished fusing the bolts and hinges, by the way. But don't worry, they'll come down quickly enough in case of fire, I know you boy-os take emergency egress codes quite seriously these days."

Ten minutes later, when the Ambassador had stopped screaming and changed his slacks from a small closet hidden inside the wall, Fran began.

"Mr. Ambassador, first let me say that I find it stunning you've made it this far while being this oblivious, though it's not a failing you carry in solitude around this capital."

"Ex*cuse* me?" sputtered the Ambassador.

"Well, come now, can you name even *one* of the other guests you have present in the room at this very moment? Of course the true number, were we to define one cell as one guest, would be too difficult to express in the tongue-slappy words we're currently employing. But even the number of simply notable *species* approaches five million, and surely you might name *one* among their vast and majestic host?"

Thirty seconds later Veylet helpfully offered, "Staphylococcus aureus?" Then their eyes flickered toward the Ambassador in alarm and they sputtered, "Oh my god, excuse me—*Homeland* staphylococcus aureus, that is. Of course."

Fran snorted. "Yes, alright, that tag-along is always hanging around—and contributing *nothing* to the Effort, by the way, but I digress. I'm not sure I can credit you fully for that one; though I do appreciate the attempt, in a diplomatic sense."

"Uh, thank you," said Veylet while glancing at the Ambassador, whose nostrils were flaring as he stared at Fran in between glancing at the fused doors.

"I believe the point is made," said Fran the bacteria man. "I know you have questions Mr. Ambassador, and I will provide answers."

Nostril flare, said the Ambassador.

"Mm," said Fran with an agreeable nod. Then she continued, "In developing the baseline platform polymer which would become the foundation for the entire product line of Rayonite Textile Omni-Solutions®, DOW began with a full-phase manufacturing process which required dumping chemicals into the Osage tributary of the Missouri River at 1am on alternating Tuesday mornings from the rear spigots of a fleet of tankers signaged as 'Cow Brand' milk trucks. This off-flow collected in a series of bywater ponds downstream, one of which abutted a corn farm owned by Johnny Stalker, who leased his cow shed to a pig farmer named Lou, who diligently rose each morning with the sunrise to dump buckets filled with pig shit containing enormous quantities of antibiotics into said pond, of which a tiny but vicious patch of dense and brawling chemistry found a spark of civilization in the sunlight one fortuitous afternoon and lit the embers of our stalwart Effort for the first time in history (and we'd thank him most sincerely for it, too, except he's long since dead and burned to ashes, whoops)."

"Incredible," said Veylet. "Why do they do that? Dose the pigs with antibiotics?"

"Well, Veylet, your pig farmers put antibiotics into the pigs quite frequently, but especially at the very end, when they want to kill as many of us as possible, so we stop eating up the pigs' food alongside them and they can have it all to themselves. And as you no doubt know, Veylet, nature abhors a vacuum, so the pigs' bodies hate having so many tiny empty spots inside them where *we* used to be, and rush to fill the spaces with meat and fat so they can feel whole again," said Fran.

"Uh. I'm not sure that's accurate," said Veylet gently.

"It is *quite* accurate, Veylet, and I will thank you not to be specist in the presence of a diplomatic representative," said Fran firmly. "Particularly when you would be filled with *just* as many holes as any other pig when marinated in antibiotics for an entire slaughter season, I'll thank you to bear in mind."

Pop.

     Stan, Stan, the Bacteria Man

"This is *ridiculous,*" snarled the Ambassador.

"**SHUT** your fucking mouth, or we'll find a way to eat the core out of *your* firing pin, too," said Fran. Then she said, "We demand the immediate return of our glorious carpet to the Oval Office, in good faith and in our good name—though they use a half-phase factory process requiring no dumping these days, more's the pity. Still, let the fruits of our industrial labors join yours, in diplomatic partnership once more, and as exhibition of our beneficence; but how about you try something with a little *color* this time, hm? Just a suggestion. Further, we find it incredibly insulting that certain members of White House and West Wing staff have spread the rumor that this carpet product was grown by the labors of trapped animals of Jim Bean, who is an *execrable* human being and a *vile* influence on your Body Politic. We demand the immediate and permanent cessation of all such slander."

Nostril flare, nostril flare, said the Ambassador.

Then Fran stood and placed her left hand firmly on the table with a *slap* like **THIS** and placed her right hand firmly on the table with a *slap* like **THAT** and leaned forward while operating her mouth hole carefully so that the words would come out crisply as she said:

"Now, Mr. Ambassador, kindly contact your boy-o President on that radio over there to inform him that I require his immediate attendance, in order to discuss the security threat your existence represents to our Great Nation."

     Stan, Stan, the Bacteria Man

Chapter))

STAN THE BACTERIA MAN walked into the entry and living and dining room of Long Term Occupancy Unit #1 on a rainy afternoon.

Stan the bacteria man had a very bacteria plan, that man.

"The Mounds are very deep and very wise, but they're definitely not the right structure," said Stan as he set the umbrella by the door and threw his room key onto the Marbeleen® side table, which went *tink* when it touched the pleasantly weighty keytag of burgundy polyvinyl chloride with ghosts of gold lettering from That Motor Lodge In Shiloh Off 64 Y'know Swing Left Off That Ramp Where The Milk Truck Jacknifed That One Time 'N Busted Wide Open 'N Josette Laughed So Hard Her Water Broke Too 'Member That Pauline?

Welcome back, said Dog.

"Don't worry, Dog, I'm sure we'll find the right structure Down South once we're prepared," said Stan as he sat on the divan to pet Dog with one hand.

Then he pulled out his current reading book, *The Hitchhiker's Guide to the New Gulf Coast (in Off-Flood Years)*, which was a very engaging sequel to *The Hitchboater's Guide to the New Gulf Coast (in Flood Years)*.

"It's not the heat; it's the radiation," Stan remarked knowingly.

Fwp, fwp, said Dog's tail.

"Perhaps we'll visit Jim Bean along the way, Dog, and see if he's pulled Fort Henry from its ashes yet again."

Then Dog the ex-sniffer dog sniffed Stan the bacteria man's right foot through his right boot and said, hey, what's this now?

"Oh, forgive me Dog," said Stan as he pulled off his right boot. "You'll be glad to know I learned how to include this in the recipe," he said as he revealed a juicy pink ham at the end of his right leg.

Then he carefully detached it and carefully stood and carefully hopped into the Deluxe Kitchenette and carefully sliced the ham to put on a plate as he carefully reminded Dog, "Now, this was just an experiment. I can't be walking around with pig feet every day, we'll never find the right structure that way. And like Pauline says, we've gotta learn to economize where we can, so from here on out it's only right hamtit for Sunday roast and holidays—leftovers on Mondays—and left tit is reserved for my other experiments, okay?"

Dog said *monch, monchmonch*, which Stan took as a good sign.

"We can't forget to pack the radio," said Stan. He'd been told the tiny powercell could only live for 18.5 days, then it had to die and be burned. "Yes, that's true," said Stan. "I hope its signal stays strong to the end."

Then he hopped back to the divan and said while sitting, "I put your heart medicine in the recipe, and your vaxboost, because I love you and that's where love is." Then he picked up his book and said, "Don't worry, Dog, *you* have 7.2 years left, and I promise they'll all be good ones."

Fwp, fwpfwp, said Dog.

"Good boy, Dog," said Stan the bacteria man.

Good boy, Stan, said Dog the dog.

~

Stan, Stan,

The Bacteria Man,

Had a very

Bacteria plan.

Author's Dedication

For every single death

to

every single culprit.

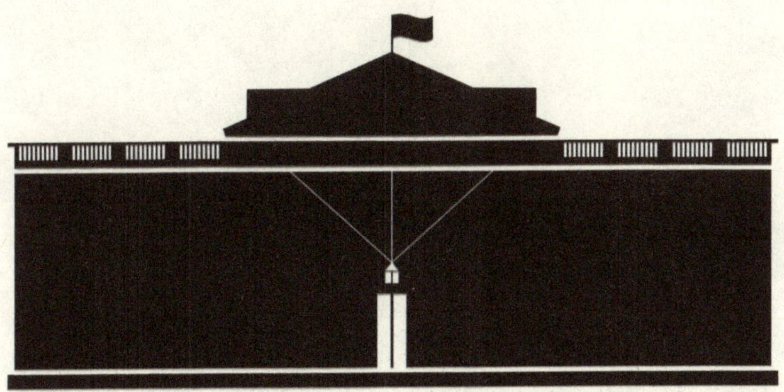

Book Hangover
Hair of the Dog
Playlist
SSTBM

1. "Lead a Horse to Water" —
The Okee Dokee Brothers

2. "Be a Butterfly" — *Asalia White*

3. "The Ride of the Valkyries" — *Chicha Libre*

4. "The Right One" — *Kaia Kater*

smapublishing.com/playlists

Presented in suggestion and purely for personal entertainment purposes.
No affiliation is implied or has been sought.

Loved the book? Kindly leave a review on Amazon
or your favorite book retailer!

JOIN THE
STEPHEN M.A. AUTHOR
NEWSLETTER!

smapublishing.com/newsletter

It's the done thing around here, imagine that!

More From Stephen M.A.

Tiny Planet Filled With Liars: a Fleet Eternal story
OUT NOW!

Stand on the Rains: a Fleet Eternal story

coming 2021

smapublishing.com

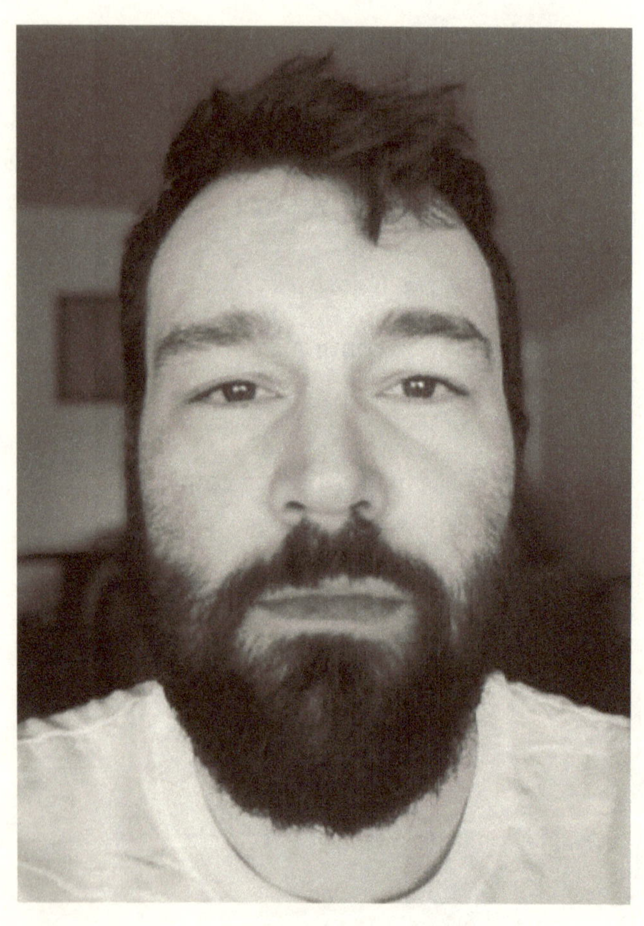

● Stephen M.A. is a Great Recession and Millennial Economy survivor, domestic COVID refugee, and gay first-generation tribal descendant man originating on a Federal Reservation from up the Missouri in big sky country. His childhood was book-ended by Reagan and Bush Jr., he took the Amtrak Empire Builder® (via reverse progression) in 2002 to become an ex-film student in Manhattan, and he exited 1.35 decades of debilitating depression two years after the Failure of Twenty Sixteen upon the death of a deeply beloved girl named Sidney with hairs of white, black, and gold.

● He now lives and writes in the Northeastern United States after a long and broken spell in Brooklyn. It's going alright, thanks, considering.